Quack Goes Camping

Written by Michèle Dufresne • Illustrated by Tracy La Rue Hohn

PIONEER VALLEY EDUCATIONAL PRESS, INC.

Mother Duck read a book
about camping to Quack
and his brother and sisters.

"I want to go camping,"
said Quack.

"Someday we will go camping,"
said Mother Duck.

SKIP
GOES
CAMPING

"I want to go camping,"
said Quack.
"I want to go swimming
in a big lake and catch fish!
I want to roast marshmallows!
I want to sleep in a tent."

"Someday we will go camping," said Mother Duck.

"I want to go camping now," said Quack.

"Someday," said Mother Duck.

In the morning,

Quack went to Mother Duck.

"Is it someday?" asked Quack.

"Can we go camping today?

I want to go swimming

in a big lake and catch fish!

I want to roast marshmallows!"

"No, not today," said Mother Duck.
"Someday we will go camping."

Quack went to find Father Duck.
"I want to go camping.
Can we go camping?
I want to go swimming
in a big lake and catch fish!
I want to roast marshmallows!
I want to sleep in a tent."

"No, not today,"
said Father Duck.
"We can go for a walk
or read a book."

"No!" said Quack.
"I want to go camping."

"You are too little
to go camping,"
said Father Duck.
"But someday we will go camping."

Quack went to Grandpa Duck.
"I want to go camping.
I am *not* too little.
I want to go swimming
in a big lake and catch fish!
I want to roast marshmallows!
I want to sleep in a tent."

"Hmm," said Grandpa Duck.
"Come with me."

Grandpa Duck and Quack
went swimming and caught fish!

They roasted marshmallows.

Then they took a nap in a tent.